THE HISTORY OF OUR HOLIDAYS

HALLOWEEN'S SPOOKY HISTORY

BY THEODORE JONES

Gareth Stevens
PUBLISHING

Please visit our website, www.garethstevens.com. For a free color catalog of all our high-quality books, call toll free 1-800-542-2595 or fax 1-877-542-2596.

Library of Congress Cataloging-in-Publication Data

Jones, Theodore (Theodore Francis), 1978-
Halloween's spooky history / Theodore Jones.
pages cm. — (The history of our holidays)
Includes bibliographical references and index.
ISBN 978-1-4824-3890-1 (pbk.)
ISBN 978-1-4824-3891-8 (6 pack)
ISBN 978-1-4824-3892-5 (library binding)
1. Halloween—Juvenile literature. I. Title.
GT4965.J66 2016
394.2646—dc23

2015018175

Published in 2016 by
Gareth Stevens Publishing
111 East 14th Street, Suite 349
New York, NY 10003

Designer: Sarah Liddell
Editor: Therese Shea

Photo credits: Cover, p. 1 Sandra Cunningham/Shutterstock.com; p. 5 YanLev/Shutterstock.com; p. 7 Globalphilosophy/Wikimedia Commons; p. 9 Dave Ethridge-Barnes/Staff/Getty Images News/Getty Images; p. 11 FastilyClone/Wikimedia Commons; pp. 12, 15 (top) File Upload Bot (Magnus Manske)/Wikimedia Commons; p. 13 Maya Kruchankova/Shutterstock.com; p. 15 (bottom) Moadhóg/Wikimedia Commons; pp. 17, 21 Monkey Business Images/Shutterstock.com; p. 19 Sean Locke Photography/Shutterstock.com.

Printed in the United States of America

CPSIA compliance information: Batch #CW16GS: For further information contact Gareth Stevens, New York, New York at 1-800-542-2595.

CONTENTS

Boldface words appear in the glossary.

Strange Holiday

Halloween can be spooky. Many people try to scare others. But it's also a fun day. People dress up in funny **costumes**. Children collect candy from neighbors. How did such a strange holiday get started? Read on to find out—if you dare!

Samhain

Many Halloween **traditions** come from the Samhain (SAH-wuhn) **festival** in Europe long ago. It took place around November 1. People believed the **souls** of the dead traveled among the living at this time. People lit fires to scare away bad spirits.

People wore costumes during Samhain so that evil spirits wouldn't know who they were. Samhain was also believed to be the time when the souls of those who had died that year traveled to a world beyond death.

All Hallows' Eve

In the 800s, the Christian holiday All Hallows' Day was moved to November 1. This was a day to honor good people called saints. All Hallows' Eve is the day before. The name "Halloween" is a short way of saying "All Hallows' Eve."

However, young people still kept up the tradition of dressing in costumes for fun around this time. They made vegetables into **lanterns** and lit them up. They carried them throughout their villages. Today, people **carve** pumpkins.

turnip lantern

Trick or Treat?

Trick-or-treating may come from England. On November 2, poor people went door to door asking for treats called "soul cakes." Later, in Scotland and Ireland, young people in costumes sang songs or told jokes for fruit, nuts, and money.

soul cakes

Today, children go trick-or-treating. They walk from house to house. At each door, they shout, "Trick or treat!" This means they'll play a trick if they don't receive a treat, often candy. Most don't play tricks, though.

A Holiday of Traditions

Many Europeans moved to the United States in the 1800s and 1900s. They brought their Halloween traditions with them, including dressing in costumes and **bobbing** for apples. Halloween became a well-loved holiday **celebrated** on October 31.

Explore Team

Halloween continues to be a mix of spooky and fun. It's a day of traditions, some from long ago and others not so old. Next October 31, put on a costume, celebrate, and remember to yell, "Trick or treat!"

GLOSSARY

bob: to try to catch a floating object with teeth

carve: to cut with care

celebrate: to honor with special activities

costume: clothes worn by someone who is trying to look like someone or something else

festival: a special time when something is celebrated

lantern: a light that can usually be carried by a handle

soul: in some beliefs, the part of a person that lives on after death

tradition: a long-practiced custom or way of life

FOR MORE INFORMATION

BOOKS

Goeller, Dorothy. *Halloween*. Berkeley Heights, NJ: Enslow Publishers, 2011.

Keogh, Josie. *Halloween*. New York, NY: PowerKids Press, 2013.

Marsh, Laura. *Halloween*. Washington, DC: National Geographic Society, 2012.

WEBSITES

Halloween

www.timeforkids.com/minisite/halloween
Check out Halloween facts and activities on this site.

History of Trick-or-Treating

www.history.com/topics/halloween/history-of-trick-or-treating
Find out more about this tradition, including customs of today.

Publisher's note to educators and parents: Our editors have carefully reviewed these websites to ensure that they are suitable for students. Many websites change frequently, however, and we cannot guarantee that a site's future contents will continue to meet our high standards of quality and educational value. Be advised that students should be closely supervised whenever they access the Internet.

INDEX